*To the women of Lake Pátzcuaro*

*For the important women in our lives: our mothers,*

ANGÉLICA AND ANGELINA,

*and the generations of strong women who came before them*

Acknowledgments

With gratitude to our friends Carmen Barnard of Morelia, Aida and
Francisco Castillejo of Erongarícuaro, Celia Pérez Ramos and
Alfredo Cortez of Tzintzuntzan for opening their homes and their hearts to us.
Thanks also to Irma Alfonso for her *buen ojo* and to Alejandro Presilla
for his contribution to the book, and to Francisca de la Luz Cortez
of Uricho for the best blue corn tortillas in the whole world.

Henry Holt and Company, Inc., *Publishers since 1866*
115 West 18th Street, New York, New York 10011
Henry Holt is a registered trademark of Henry Holt and Company, Inc.
Published in Canada by Fitzhenry & Whiteside Ltd.,
195 Allstate Parkway, Markham, Ontario L3R 4T8.

Library of Congress Cataloging-in-Publication Data
Presilla, Maricel E. Life around the lake: the feasts of Lake Pátzcuaro /
by Maricel E. Presilla and Gloria Soto.
Summary: Depicts how the Tarascan embroiderers around Lake
Pátzcuaro in central Mexico are adapting to modern life.
1. Tarasco embroidery—Juvenile literature.    2. Tarasco Indians—Social life and
customs—Juvenile literature.    3. Pátzcuaro, Lake (Mexico)—Social life and
customs.—Juvenile literature. [1. Tarasco Indians—Social life and customs.
2. Indians of Mexico—Social life and customs.]    I. Soto, Gloria.    II. Title.
F1221.T3P73    1996    972'.37—dc20    95-38429

ISBN 0-8050-3800-0
First Edition—1996
Printed in the United States of America on acid-free paper.∞
1 3  5  7  9  10  8  6  4  2

# Life Around the Lake

## MARICEL E. PRESILLA and GLORIA SOTO

## Embroideries by the Women of Lake Pátzcuaro

HENRY HOLT AND COMPANY • NEW YORK

*"When we show the lake in our embroideries, we want people to see it as beautiful, the way it used to be, with its many fish."*

Lake Pátzcuaro is a lake of volcanic origin nourished by rainwater. It is located midway between the cities of Morelia and Uruapan, in the green and fertile state of Michoacán in west-central Mexico. The women of Tzintzuntzan call Lake Pátzcuaro "the jewel of Michoacán."

For many centuries, Tarascan Indians have lived in towns like Tzintzuntzan along the shores of Lake Pátzcuaro. *Tzintzuntzan (tseen-TSOON-tsahn)* means "the place of the hummingbirds," and the sound of the word is like the buzz of the birds' tiny wings.

The lake gave the Tarascans fish to eat and reeds to weave into baskets and mats. From the lake they also took water for drinking and for tending their cornfields. The lake is still large and beautiful, dotted with five islands and surrounded by green fields of corn and alfalfa. High mountains—once active volcanoes—rise close to its shores, and white clouds cast their cottony shadows on the steel-gray waters.

But the people who live in the nearby towns and ranches know the lake is in danger. They can see heavy rains washing soil from the treeless mountains into the water, filling the lake. They also know that pollution is killing fish and making the lake's waters dangerous to drink.

The old remember when wild ducks swam noisily among the reeds. Then, when the lake was wider and deeper and its waters blue, clean, and fresh, fishermen's nets brimmed with precious whitefish.

The women from the town of Tzintzuntzan and nearby Santa Cruz Ranch recall those happy times in their colorful embroideries. In this way, they honor the past and also make a living today.

This is the story of the lake and the life of the people who live around it, as told by their embroideries.

*"Without water, there is no life."*

—JOSÉ GUADALUPE

Every afternoon as the sun goes down, José Guadalupe follows its golden trail, paddling his boat to the lake's hidden coves and deep waters. All night he sits quietly in his wooden boat taking care of his *agallera,* a large net used to catch *pescado blanco* (whitefish). He has nets of many kinds for different uses. Some are large and wide, and they are called *chinchorros.* Others, called *mariposas,* are small and shaped like the wings of butterflies ready to take flight.

Sometimes José Guadalupe returns home empty-handed. But when he is lucky, he moors his boat at the pier of *Ojo del agua* (Eye of the

Water) at the crack of dawn and unloads full nets. He may have golden carp and large tilapia, tiny fish called *charales* and *pescado blanco,* a fish so transparent one can even see its delicate bones.

*Lago de Pátzcuaro*

**Lake Pátzcuaro**

*"When I was small I would go to the pier, and I would see fishermen bring in large fish and small ones. But little by little, they have gone, they have gone, the fish have gone. I think it is because the lake is very dirty, or because we have not been careful with the lake."*

—POMPOSA RENDÓN

In the afternoon, when his nets are dried, José Guadalupe sits quietly on a stool to mend them or to weave new ones. He feels fortunate, for he is still able to make a living as a fisherman, like his father, and his grandfather before him. He knows that the fishermen of Puácuaro—another town on the other side of the lake—are not able to catch fish anymore. Instead of fishing, they have had to find work weaving baskets and mats.

*El pescador*
The Fisherman

*Artesanos en Michoacán*

**Artisans of Michoacán**

*"There are fishermen, and there are artisans who find their materials in the lake. Our ancestors left these crafts as their gifts to us. We are poor. But because of what we can make from the lake, we are not as poor as people in other places. Life is easier here. We have the wealth that the lake brings us."*

—DARÍA PEÑA VILLAGÓMEZ

Celia, Marta, Daría, and many other women in Tzintzuntzan sell their embroideries in the town's craft market. If you look closely at this embroidery you can see other Michoacán artisans at work. The potters of Tzintzuntzan make delicate white ceramics decorated with painted scenes of the lake. The town also has many expert wood and stone carvers.

In other towns women weave their striped blue, white, and black *rebozos* (shawls), while men make brightly colored ponchos called *jorongos*. The men of the island of Jarácuaro also make tightly woven hats from palm fibers. In nearby Puácuaro, families make baskets from lake grasses such as *tule* and *chuspata* that are used to keep tortillas warm.

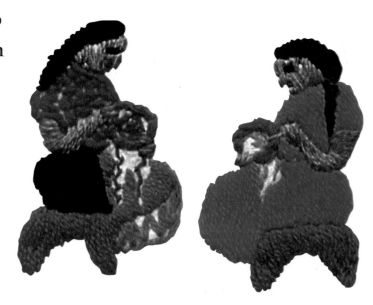

Santa Cruz Ranch is like a town, but it does not have a central square, paved streets, or a large church. Each family lives in a small house with some land around it to raise pigs, chickens, and perhaps a cow.

Around the ranch there are cornfields. The men go to work early in the morning and do not return until sundown. When beans and pumpkins are planted alongside corn, the fields are called *milpas*. The combination of these plants helps keep the soil rich and strong.

Edelia Barriga, who made this embroidery, wakes up before the roosters and begins to cook for her family. She cooks beans in a round clay pot, seasoning them with lard and a tasty, aromatic herb called *epazote*. While she waits for the beans to soften, she kneads corn dough (*masa*) to make fresh tortillas. When the food is ready, Edelia and the other women of the ranch take it to the men in the cornfields. During the autumn harvest, families prepare corn feasts called *elotadas* in the fields. The women boil corn on the cob and make delicate fresh corn tamales called *uchepos*.

When their many chores are done, the women can work on the colorful embroideries that describe life around the lake.

*Este es mi ranchito, chiquito pero bonito.*

**This Is My Small but Beautiful Ranch.**

Everything tastes especially delicious when wrapped in the fresh corn tortillas sold door to door by Francisca de la Luz Cortez. She uses the corn grown by her husband in a *milpa* that stretches from the back of her house to the shores of Lake Pátzcuaro.

Not everybody makes tortillas by hand nowadays, but Francisca is an expert. Her tiny hands move as fast as the wings of a hummingbird as she pats down the small ball of *masa* with a flip-flap sound. Before you know it, she turns the lump of *masa* into a perfectly thin and flat tortilla. Then with a special turn of the wrist that only comes from years of experience, she sets the tortilla on the hot clay *comal* (griddle) that rests on top of a wood fire. When

the tortilla puffs once, she turns it over and waits a few seconds. Then she takes it from the griddle and places it in a basket covered with a napkin to keep it warm.

*Las cocineras de Michoacán*
The cooks of Michoacán

*Boda en el lago de Pátzcuaro*

Marriage near Lake Pátzcuaro

Though Tarascan people work very hard, they also have many dances and feasts. In the lake area, weddings are celebrated on Saturday mornings. After the church ceremony, the bride and groom and their wedding party dance their way through the streets of the town to have breakfast at the house of the best man. There they eat *pozole,* a type of stew made with hominy, and drink *atole,* which is a hot and creamy corn *masa* gruel. At noon, they again dance to the groom's house, where a great banquet awaits them.

Once there, the couple sit together with family and friends at a long table; they enjoy a vegetable soup followed by boiled chicken doused in aromatic *mole.* The *mole* is a thick and spicy sauce made with several types of chiles and dozens of other ingredients. At weddings, it is served with delicious rice.

After lunch everyone gets ready to do the Dance of the Sea Snake (*Danza de la víbora de la mar*). The bride and groom stand up on chairs opposite each other. The groom holds the bride's veil as if it were a bridge. The female friends of the bride snake their way under the veil followed by the male friends of the groom. For Alfredo Cortez of Tzintzuntzan, the dance has only one meaning—happiness.

*"An old man is like a baby learning to walk—it looks like he is falling over. Then you find a way to help him by giving him what we call a burro, a cane."*

—NICOLÁS CONSTANTINO

A much-loved dance in the Lake Pátzcuaro area is the *Danza de los viejitos* (Dance of the Old Men). Each town has its own version and a special date on which it is performed. In Jarácuaro, the town of the hatmakers, the dance is part of the feast of Saint Peter, held on June 29. People line the streets of Jarácuaro to watch a small group of men dance their way through town tapping their sandals to the sound of music. Under their wide hats they wear comic masks portraying grimacing, toothless, white-skinned old men. The dancers are dressed in the traditional Tarascan fashion of white pants trimmed in red and blue *jorongos*. Leading them are three musicians playing guitar, violin, and bass. As they dance, they hunch over and hold their canes as if they were very old men. As the music speeds up they tap faster and faster. In one dance called *El trenecito*, the music and the tapping sound like a train.

Dance master Nicolás Constantino thinks he knows why the dancers wear white masks. He explains that the Tarascans noticed that Spanish men aged faster than Indian men, and so they invented this dance as a way to make fun of the aging conquistadores.

*La danza de los viejitos*

The Dance of the Old Men

In early June, all the workers of Tzintzuntzan get together for the great Catholic feast of Corpus Christi. For Catholics, the body of Christ—Corpus Christi—symbolizes the community in which all share. This feast is a time for giving.

The feast begins early in the morning when people gather under the tower of the four-hundred-year-old Franciscan church to catch the fruits and gifts that are thrown down. Children jump trying to grab whatever they can.

The *yunteros,* or the farmers who till the soil with their plows, come to town with their oxen beautifully decked with ribbons and flowers. The *arrieros,* who every day of the year bring loads of vegetables and wood on their donkeys, gather to cook in the atrium of the church amid ancient olive trees. In large blackened pots they make an aromatic *atole* spiced with bay leaves. They kneel on the floor to grind *nixtamal,* corn that has been boiled in water and lime to remove its skin. Then they cook fresh corn tortillas on a clay *comal.* Everyone comes with their own clay cups to drink the *arriero*'s *atole* and to savor the piping hot tortillas.

From nearby *Ojo del agua* comes a noisy parade. The fishermen hold a large *chinchorro* net, and they dance while pretending to catch a large fish. It is not really a fish they are after, though, but a man wearing a large papier-mâché fish on his head. The women dance all around him carrying baskets filled with golden fried fish. The smell is inviting and the music happy and lively. Everyone in town rushes to meet the *Danza del pescado* (Dance of the Fish).

*La fiesta del Corpus Christi en Tzintzuntzan*

The Feast of Corpus Christi in Tzintzuntzan

*La fiesta del Corpus Christi en Tzintzuntzan*

The Feast of Corpus Christi in Tzintzuntzan

In one corner of the church's atrium, potters have been busy since dawn firing small clay pots in a large makeshift adobe oven. These will be given away as gifts. Women sit nearby stirring big pots filled with flavorful *mole.*

The night before the Corpus Christi, the town's hunters search for rabbits to cook in a green *mole* flavored with pickled jalapeño peppers. The hunt takes them to the hills near town and to the *yacatas.* Step pyramids made of large stone blocks, the *yacatas* were built by the Tarascans long before the Spaniards came to the lakeshore in the early sixteenth century. Tzintzuntzan was the capital of the Tarascan empire, and the five *yacatas* here are the largest and most impressive in the lake area.

On the day of the Corpus Christi, children have fun dressing like *huacaleros* (people who carry heavy loads on their backs). They also have an especially wonderful time playing a game called the *palo encebado* (greased pole). A tall, thick wooden pole is set in the ground and crowned with gifts for those who can reach them. But the pole has been smeared with fat, and anyone who tries to climb to the top slides down, making everyone laugh.

*"I remember the dead, that's why I come. Why not? That's why we are here. People say they will come, and we will stay here all night with them. . . . I was born here, I was raised here, and here in this cemetery I will remain."*

—IRENE ZAVALA CARRILLO

When the last rains of autumn turn the fields emerald-green, white and yellow flowers sprout on the sides of the road that circles the lake. Then, the people of Tzintzuntzan prepare to honor their dead.

Irene Zavala Carrillo and other women gather at the town's two cemeteries to pull out the tall weeds that blanket the simple, mounded earth tombs of their loved ones. Between October 31 and November 2, these tombs will gleam anew with the bright colors of orange marigolds and scarlet cockspurs. Among the flowers covering the tombs of two of her children, Irene places white candles and a basket filled with fruits and *pan de muerto,* a delicate anise-scented bread molded into many shapes.

Tall and colorful arches garlanded with marigolds head other tombs. The arch is the Christmas tree of the dead, and it is trimmed with sugar skulls, fruits, and more *pan de muerto.*

When evening falls on October 31, the tombs of Tzintzuntzan's two cemeteries—one on each side of the main street—glow with the flickering

light of hundreds of candles. It is the Vigil of the Little Angels. Next to the tombs of their dead children, whole families sit on straw mats, huddled together to keep warm. They sit very closely to those they still love so much, and they spend the whole night in vigil, awake.

Many years ago, the Days of the Dead were family feasts. Today people from all over Mexico and even from abroad come to Tzintzuntzan to be a part of this beautiful celebration. On November 1, when the town's cemeteries and the *yacatas* are ablaze with candlelight, Tzintzuntzan bustles with the sounds of a lively fair.

All through the night, the women take turns selling their embroideries at the craft market. The tempting aroma of *pozole* and hot fruit punch fills the air. Loud music often deafens the prayers of the mourners in the town cemeteries, but soft and soothing Tarascan love songs called *pirekuas* can also be heard through the night.

*La noche de los muertos*
The Night of the Dead

# The Embroiderers of Tzintzuntzan

When we first traveled to the Lake Pátzcuaro area, we were drawn to the colorful embroideries sold by a guild of women artisans in Tzintzuntzan. The first piece we collected was strikingly beautiful and stood out from the others. It showed a trio of dark-haired Tarascan women holding a basket of fruit on their heads; their image was surrounded by a colorful border. We later learned that this design, used time and again by many embroiderers, was first sketched by a Tzintzuntzan man named Alfredo Cortez to be embroidered by his wife, Celia Pérez Ramos.

Alfredo explained to us that he had been inspired by a sculpture that stands at the base of the imposing aqueduct of Morelia, the capital of the state of Michoacán. But for us, the three Tarascans in the embroidery will always stand for the strong and hard-working women that we met around the lake.

The first organized guild of embroiderers in Tzintzuntzan, appropriately called *El grupo colibrí* or The Hummingbird Group, was started about fourteen years ago by Annemieke Thijsse. The teacher, or *la maestra* as she is still affectionately remembered by the women, taught them to apply their skill in embroidery to themes from Tarascan mythology drawn from ancient seals found in Tzintzuntzan.

*Las Tarascas de Michoacán*
~~~~~~~~~~~~~~~~~~~~~
The Tarascan Women of Michoacán

The first formal exhibition of the group's work took place at the Museo Regional de Artes Populares in Pátzcuaro in May 1981. The majority of the pieces exhibited—with few exceptions—were modeled after the abstract patterns of Tarascan art. But gradually the women began depicting scenes of life around the lake.

There are two groups of embroiderers in Tzintzuntzan—the original Colibrí group, led by Daría Peña, and the unnamed but smaller group led by Celia Pérez, who works in close collaboration with her husband. The other members of Celia's group take turns bringing their pieces to sell at the craft market.

At nearby Santa Cruz Ranch, two large and prolific groups of embroiderers—mostly members of the extended Barriga family—are also busy at work. Edelia Barriga, the creator of one of our favorite pieces, "Este es mi ranchito, chiquito pero bonito," is the leader of one of the groups.

All the women embroiderers of the Lake Pátzcuaro area continue to keep their traditions alive by teaching these crafts to their children.

The women of both Tzintzuntzan and Santa Cruz are aware of the role of their work in preserving the history and traditions of Lake Pátzcuaro. It was by talking to these women time and again that we began to realize our book must deal not only with the activities depicted in the embroideries but the threats to their way of life.

All the Tzintzuntzan embroiderers had something revealing to share about the lake's current situation. They are angry that poor drainage and lack of sewage treatment have polluted the lake. They are alarmed that fish introduced to the lake, like carp and tilapia, are now competing with prized native species like whitefish. They are saddened that

well-intentioned efforts to drag the lake to make it deeper have resulted in the uprooting of valuable aquatic grasses such as *tule*.

Daría Peña believes that education is the key to solving the lake's problems. Voicing the feelings of other women in town, she suggests that schools should be more aggressive in teaching children how to save the lake. Daría herself has participated in several campaigns to reforest the lake area.

What the women of Tzintzuntzan have seen for themselves is echoed by Ada Castillejo, an anthropologist who has dedicated years of research to the lake basin area. Through many conversations with Dr. Castillejo and her brother Francisco Castillejo, an ecologist who lives in Eronguarícuaro, we realized the extent of the lake's problems. But what the professionals and the women have in common is their belief that there is hope for renewal through adaptation and awareness.

Over the centuries much has changed in the Lake Pátzcuaro basin: the Tarascans were conquered by the Spaniards; the Franciscans came and brought Christianity and new crafts; the lake is now threatened by pollution and neglect; lake people have to find alternative ways to make a living; and the Days of the Dead have a commercial side that did not exist before. But still the people of Lake Pátzcuaro prevail. Both the noisy market and the dignified vigil at Tzintzuntzan's cemeteries nourish the life of the town and its people. The women embroiderers recognize these changes and through their work help build a better future.

# Pronunciation Guide

agallera    *ah-gah-LYAY-rah*

arrieros    *ah-rree-AY-rohs*

artesanos    *ar-teh-SAH-nohs*

atole    *ah-TOH-leh*

boda    *BOH-dah*

charales    *chah-RAH-lehs*

chinchorros    *cheen-CHOH-rrohs*

chuspata    *choos-PAH-tah*

comal    *koh-MAHL*

cocineras    *coh-see-NAY-rahs*

Danza de los viejitos
    *DAHN-sah deh lohs vee-eh-HEE-tohs*

El grupo colibrí    *ehl GROO-poh koh-lee-BREE*

El pescador    *ehl peh-scah-DOHR*

El trenecito    *ehl trehn-eh-SEE-toh*

elotadas    *eh-loh-TAH-dahs*

epazote    *eh-pah-SOH-teh*

Eronguarícuaro    *eh-rohn-gwah-REE-kwah-roh*

Este es mi ranchito, chiquito pero bonito
    *EH-steh ehs mee rahn-CHEE-toh,*
    *chee-KEE-toh peh-roh boh-NEE-toh*

huacaleros    *wahk-ah-LAY-rohs*

Jarácuaro    *hah-RAH-kwah-roh*

jorongos    *hoh-ROHN-gohs*

la danza    *lah DAHN-sah*

la fiesta    *lah fee-EH-stah*

la maestra    *lah mah-EH-strah*

la mar    *lah MAHR*

la noche    *lah NOH-cheh*

la víbora    *lah VEE-boh-rah*

los muertos    *lohs mooEHR-tohs*

mariposas    *mah-ree-POH-sahs*

masa    *MAH-sah*

Michoacán    *mee-choh-ah-CAHN*

milpas    *MEEL-pahs*

mole    *MOH-leh*

Morelia    *moh-RAY-Lee-ah*

Museo Regional de Artes Populares
    *moo-SAY-oh ray-hee-oh-NAHL*
    *deh AHR-tehs poh-poo-LAH-rehs*

nixtamal    pronounced *neeks-tah-MAHL*
    in Pátzcuaro; elsewhere in Mexico,
    *neesh-tah-MAHL*

Ojo del agua    *OH-ho dehl AH-gwah*

palo encebado    *PAH-loh ehn-seh-BAH-doh*

pan de muerto    *PAHN deh moo-EHR-toh*

Pátzcuaro    *PAHT-skwah-roh*

pescado blanco    *pehs-KAH-doh BLAHN-koh*

pirekuas    *pee-REH-koo-ahs*

pozole    *poh-SOH-leh*

Puácuaro    *PWAH-kwah-roh*

rebozos    *reh-BOH-sohs*

Santa Cruz    *SAHN-tah CROOS*

tamales    *tah-MAH-lehs*

Tarascans    *tah-RAH-scahns*

tortillas    *tor-TEE-lyahs*

tule    *TOO-leh*

Tzintzuntzan    *tseen-TSOON-tsahn*

uchepos    *oo-CHEH-pohs*

Uricho    *oo-REE-choh*

Uruapan    *oo-roo-AH-pahn*

yacatas    *yah-CAH-tahs*

yunteros    *yoon-TAY-rohs*